CRUNCHY CARROTS

CRUNCHY CARROTS

Carrots of Wisdom for Little Ones

Ten short tales from Henry the Great Blue Heron
in the garden, where his critter friends play, laugh,
and learn a few of life's lessons along the way.

Written by
SONDRA PERRY

Illustrated by Janice Byer
Edited by Jennifer Redovian

MCP Books
322 First Avenue N., 5th floor
Minneapolis MN 55401
612455.2293
www.mcpbooks.com

Illustrated by Janice Byer
Edited by Jennifer Redovian
Design by Val Sherer
Photo of Henry the Heron by Sondra Perry
A portion of every book sold goes to
Shepherd's Gate Shelter for Women and Children in Livermore, CA.

www.KidsCarrotsBookSeries.com
ISBN 978-1-63505-140-7
LCCN: 2016908561
Distributed by Itasca Books
Printed in the United States of America

To Henry and all the blessed critters and birds that grace
our planet. Life would not be the same without you.
Celebrate and enjoy nature everyday!

Contents

8

Introduction

Welcome! I'm Henry, a great blue heron, here in the Perry family's backyard. I am a bird. A very big bird. I am four feet tall, and when I fly, my wings stretch six feet across.

My eyes are yellow and I have a white cap of fur on top of my head that sometimes sticks straight up. My feathers are mostly blue and gray, some are brown and white. My beak is like a long, sharp spear, which is great for fishing. Fish is my favorite, but I also eat snakes, mice, and gophers too!

I live nearby, but spend lots of time here in the Perry's backyard. I have been visiting for thirteen years. It's a great place to hang out. Many other birds and critters are here too, they are my friends. The Perry's take good care of us all. There's plenty of food, water, and shelter.

The Perry's think of me as their *pet.* You can read, *The Most Unusual Pet Ever: Henry Our Great Blue Heron and His Adventures* to find out all about that.

For now, let's go have some fun! Come with me to meet some of my friends as we play, laugh, and learn some of life's lessons along the way.

Mother Missed It

The past is already gone and the future is not here yet. But the present...is happening now. Sometimes we get so caught up about what happened in the past or what we think will happen in the future, that we lose sight of the most important time of all, the present.

It's early in the morning and Mother, one of the three chickens that live in the Perry's garden, is in a tizzy.

"Why didn't you let me sleep in? I need my beauty rest for the party tonight. Now look at me!" Mother squawks at Raven and Braveheart, the other two chickens in the coop.

"I don't know why you're squawking at us," Raven says. "You're a chicken, and chickens get up with the sun. We always have and always will. You can take a nap later."

"What's the big deal anyway?" asks Braveheart.

"You know I've been invited to Hoot Owl's Full Moon Party tonight. It's quite an honor," Mother replies, proudly. "I've always wanted to go, but chickens aren't usually invited because we're not night-time critters. But

Hoot Owl says that I have lived here long enough to be included in the fun."

"You're going to stay up all night to look at the full moon with an owl, raccoons, mice, and a bunch of bats? Have fun with that," Braveheart says, hopping out of the coop to join Raven heading toward the garden.

Suddenly Mother notices that a few of her feathers are out of place.

"Look! My feathers are all ruffled. This simply will not do. I need to look my best for tonight," Mother squawks loudly as she spins around checking every angle. "Get out of my way! I have to get water from the pond and

fix this ruffled mess," she clucks, pushing past Raven and Braveheart.

Mother grumbles all the way through the garden to the pond.

Meanwhile, as the sun slowly begins to rise, the sky is filled with glowing, tangled wisps of orange and yellow. Raven and Braveheart stop to look in awe. In fact, all the critters in the garden become still

as they take in the wonderful sight.

"The sunrise is one of nature's many presents," Braveheart says to a group of little songbirds, quietly staring up at the sky. "Mother will want to see this."

"Mother, look at this magnificent sunrise!" Braveheart calls out, trying to get her attention.

Mother is too busy to look. She's still at the pond fussing over her feathers and her big night out.

"What a beautiful sunrise," the songbirds chirp softly.

Mother missed it.

A few minutes later, as Raven scratches in the dirt looking for bugs to eat, she hears a loud humming sound and tilts her head up to see what it is.

"Look at all the hummingbirds! How cool is that?" Raven cries out.

The colorful, delicate birds have gathered, waiting their turn to smell the amazing red rose.

"That rose wasn't here yesterday. It must have bloomed this morning when the sun came up. It's the first rose to bloom this year," Raven says to Braveheart excitedly. "It's so big! And red! I bet it smells good too. No wonder all the hummingbirds are here. Let's go tell Mother. She'll want to see this flower and all the hummingbirds. They won't stay long."

"Mother, Mother! You have to come see this," Raven and Braveheart cluck together, running up to Mother who is still at the pond trying to fix her feathers.

"Leave me alone! I told you both, I don't have time to look today," she shouts.

"Okay, okay," say Raven and Braveheart, shaking their heads.

"What a wonderful sight those hummingbirds make waiting to smell the first rose," Raven says to Braveheart.

Mother missed it.

On their way back through the garden, the two chickens notice three baby robins perched on the edge of their nest.

"Oh my gosh! Look, the robins are finally ready to take their first flight and leave the nest," says Braveheart frantically. "Mother *really* needs to see this. She's been asking them every day when they will fly from their nest. She'd want to say good-bye."

"Mother, Mother! You have to come see this," Braveheart yells, running up to Mother, who is now busy giving herself a dust bath.

"I told you not to bother me today. I don't have time!" Mother scowls.

"Okay," Braveheart says softly, backing away from Mother.

At that moment, the three baby robins flap their wings and leave their nest.

As they fly over the fence, they call back to Raven and Braveheart, "Say good-bye to Mother for us!"

"We will," Raven and Braveheart reply sadly.

Mother missed it.

Late that night Mother returns from Hoot Owl's Full Moon Party.

"That was not what I expected," she mutters to herself, as the other two chickens are asleep. "It's dark and cold out there. I'm so tired. I just want to get in the coop and go to sleep. What chicken stays up this late anyway?"

In the morning Mother awakens and looks around the garden. "When did the red rose bloom? Did the hummingbirds show up to smell it? Where are the baby robins? Did they leave their nest?" she says anxiously.

"We tried to get your attention yesterday," says Raven, as Braveheart nods in agreement.

"I spent my whole day fretting about the party. I missed so much," Mother coos softly. "But not anymore. I don't want to miss anything else. Starting right now. Come on girls! The sun is shining brightly, and there are big white fluffy clouds in the sky. It's going to be a great day, and I'm not going to miss a thing."

Every day nature brings little gifts our way. A beautiful sunrise filling the sky with color, a line of hummingbirds gathering to smell a flower, or robins flying from their nest. These are the things that are happening right now. Never get so busy that you miss the presents of today.

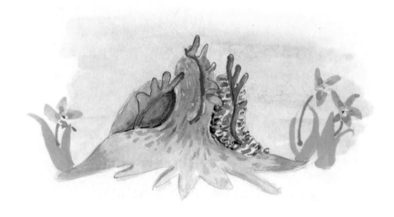

Don't Fall for It

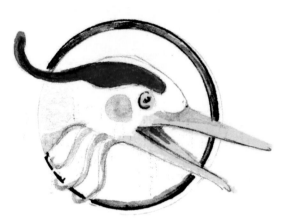

Critters often make up stories and say things in fun. But remember, just because a critter says something, it doesn't automatically make it true. You get to decide, based on what you know to be true in your head and in your heart, whether or not to believe their words.

It's a cold, crisp morning. Blue Jay and the resident chickens, Mother, Raven, and Braveheart, are busy grooming themselves.

"I can't wait for the sun to shine on the window so I can see my reflection," Raven

says, standing in front of the dark-shaded glass. "It's easier to groom my shiny black feathers when I can see them."

Blue Jay suddenly gets a twinkle in his eye. Knowing that Raven cannot see her reflection in the window until the sun rises above the tall trees and shines on the glass, he decides to tease her. He gives a quick wink to Braveheart and Mother, letting them know something is up.

"Hey, Raven, why are your feathers red?" Blue Jay asks slyly.

"My feathers are not red!" huffs Raven.

"Yes, all the feathers on top of your head and down your back are red," Blue Jay declares.

Raven turns to Mother and Braveheart. "Are my feathers red or black? Tell me the truth!" she demands.

"Oh they are red. Bright red in fact," Mother says, with half a smile, turning quickly to avoid giving the joke away.

Raven strains her eyes and looks closer into the window. But she still can't see her reflection. She anxiously twists her head around to inspect the feathers on her back.

"I don't want red feathers! How will I get my shiny black feathers back? How did this happen?" Raven cries out.

Blue Jay, Mother, and Braveheart start to giggle softly at Raven's innocent behavior. She is falling for their words.

"In just a few minutes when the sun comes up over the treetops, you will be laughing too," Braveheart whispers in Raven's ear, trying not to laugh out loud.

Raven stands by the window and waits patiently, squinting her eyes, anxious to catch the first glimpse of her reflection in the window. When the sun finally

rises over the treetops and shines on the window, Raven is ready.

"I knew it! I knew my feathers were not red! I know who I am and what color my feathers are. I can't believe I fell for their words!" Raven proclaims.

Raven starts to laugh along with her friends. Mostly she is laughing at herself.

Raven realized how silly it is to believe something another critter says over what she knows to be true in her head and in her heart. From now on, she will think first and then decide whether or not to fall for it.

Stay With Me!

It's important to respect that different critters have different needs, even if you don't understand the reasons behind them. What is best for one might not be best for the other. Little Squirrel learns this lesson one winter when he talks Little Turtle into staying above ground with him instead of doing what she normally does, hibernate.

Winter is coming. The air is crisp. The trees are losing their leaves, and the ground is becoming cold. All the critters in the Perry's garden are preparing themselves for the frosty months ahead. Some critters prepare a nest or burrow, and others, like Little Turtle, dig a hole in the ground to hibernate.

Little Turtle is having a hard time getting her best friend, Little Squirrel, to understand this.

"Hi Little Squirrel!" says Little Turtle cheerfully. "I see you're gathering acorns for the winter. I have my hibernation spot all picked out. Later today, I'll dig a hole big enough for me, and tomorrow I'll get in it and cover myself up with dirt. That's where I'll stay through the winter. You know that I'm going to miss you, but we'll be back together in the spring."

Little Squirrel stops hiding his acorns and turns to look at Little Turtle.

"So...like...you dig a deep hole and go in it for the entire winter?" asks Little Squirrel. "You said earlier that your breathing gets slow and you don't eat. Unbelievable! I just don't get it," Little Squirrel moans.

"Remember, I told you that turtles need to hibernate in the winter for our safety. It's the way our bodies are made," Little Turtle explains, hoping to get Little Squirrel to understand.

"You'll miss the winter fun. It will be so boring without you. I'll miss you!" says Little Squirrel.

"I'll miss you too!" replies Little Turtle. "But what can I do?"

"You just can't leave me. What will I do without you. Please don't go! Please stay. Please. Why can't you stay with me above ground? You might even like being out in winter like I do. I'll take care of you," Little Squirrel pleads.

"I would like to play the games you talk about. And I've never seen the snow. It might not be a bad thing," Little Turtle says quietly, putting her head down.

"Please! Please!" Little Squirrel begs. "Stay with me!"

After a long pause, Little Turtle lifts her head up and cries, "Okay, I will! I'll stay with you for the winter!"

The friends hug tightly.

"You'll see. We'll have the best time! Better than sleeping in a hole," Little Squirrel says happily.

The weeks go by and winter settles in. Little Squirrel shows Little Turtle how to slide across the ice, but Little Turtle cracks her shell skidding into the fence. The acorns Little Squirrel shares with Little Turtle are too hard for her to digest. When the temperature drops and her body slows down, Little Turtle can no longer keep up with Little Squirrel.

One morning Little Squirrel cannot find Little Turtle.

"Have you seen Little Turtle?" he's been asking the critters all day. "Have you seen her? Where can she be?"

Late that afternoon the search is over.

"Hey! Come here quick!" Bunny shouts from the yard next door.

Little Squirrel runs over to find Little Turtle lying limp on the ground. Her head and legs are sticking out of her shell.

"Oh no. She is so weak. I've got to do something!" Little Squirrel yells. Suddenly he remembers what Little Turtle told him about hibernating and begins to dig frantically. "I'll dig a deep hole, put her in it, and cover her up so she can hibernate for the rest of the winter."

When Little Squirrel is done, all he can do is wait for spring and hope that Little Turtle will be okay. He checks the spot where she is every day.

Spring finally arrives.

Early one sunny morning, as Little Squirrel approaches the spot, he sees Little Turtle slowly emerging from her hole. He squeaks with excitement and jumps into the air. Then he settles down and nestles closely beside Little Turtle.

"I'm so sorry. I didn't understand how important hibernating is for you. I should have let you do what you needed to do, even if I didn't understand," Little Squirrel says anxiously. "Tell me, what was it like down there? Could you hear anything? Are you hungry? Are you okay?"

"I feel great. You saved me! You dug the perfect hole for me. I'll tell you about my hibernation *after* you tell me what you did for the rest of the winter," Little Turtle replies.

"Okay, but will you let me dig your hibernation hole every year?" Little Squirrel asks.

"You bet!" Little Turtle says joyfully.

The two friends scurry away to share their winter-time stories.

From that day on, Little Squirrel and Little Turtle's friendship was stronger than ever. They gained respect and compassion for each other's differences. Both realized that what is best for one of them may not be the best for the other.

It's Not About You

It's easy to jump to the wrong conclusion when we try to guess the reason behind a critter's behavior, especially when we don't have the whole story. Sometimes we might even start to believe that we are responsible for how a critter is behaving. Not having the full story leads a flock of turkeys to do just that.

The turkeys gobble gobble as they wander through the neighborhood.

"Let's hop the fence and visit the Perry's garden," says the eldest turkey. "We haven't been there in a while, and I'd like to drink from the waterfall."

All the turkeys gobble in agreement and begin hopping over the fence, one by one, into the Perry's garden.

As the turkeys walk toward the waterfall, their friend Butterfly abruptly approaches, flitting wildly from side to side above them and then disappears as fast as she had arrived.

"Hey, did you see that? Butterfly almost hit me in the head! I think she needs a flying lesson," huffs the littlest turkey. "Then she just left and didn't even say hello or good-bye."

"What did we do?" all the turkeys wonder.

The flock begins drinking from the waterfall when they notice Bun-Bun the bunny on the other side of the garden.

"Hello Bun-Bun!" the eldest turkey calls

out, waving his wing.

Bun-Bun is pacing back and forth; she looks up but doesn't reply and then hops away.

"What was that all about?" the eldest turkey asks aloud. "Didn't she see us? She looked right at us."

The turkeys shake their heads.

"What did we do?" all the turkeys wonder.

The rhythm of fast, fluttering wings fills the air. Hummingbird is flying toward the flock. The turkeys look up and wave.

"I haven't seen Hummingbird for so long. I bet he's heading for his favorite feeder," says one of the flock. "There he goes, right past us!

"He flew right out of the garden without even saying hello!" exclaims the eldest turkey.

"What did we do?" all the turkeys wonder.

The littlest turkey asks, "Did...we do something to make Butterfly, Bun-Bun, and Hummingbird not like us?"

"Do we smell bad?" one of the other turkeys blurts out.

"Did we offend someone on our last visit?" another turkey asks aloud.

Dismayed, all the turkeys want to move to a different garden and begin heading toward the fence to leave.

Suddenly Bun-Bun appears, hopping toward the flock. "Hey turkeys, where are you going?" she calls out. "You just got here."

Butterfly and Hummingbird fly into the garden and join Bun-Bun standing next to the turkeys.

The eldest turkey stops, turns around, and replies, "Sorry Bun-Bun but we're not feeling welcomed. When we arrived you looked right at us but acted like you didn't see us. Then, Butterfly nearly flew into littlest turkey's head. And just now Hummingbird flew right past us without saying hi or bye. What did we do wrong?"

"Oh no!" Bun-Bun quickly replies. "When you saw me earlier, one of my little bunnies had just gotten away from me. I found her, but I was in quite a panic."

"Oh, we didn't know," says the flock quietly.

Butterfly adds, "I tore my wing on a thorny rose bush and lost control of my flying. I'm sorry littlest turkey. I didn't mean to fly so close to your head."

"Oh, we didn't know," says the flock quietly.

Then says Hummingbird, "I travel a long way to get here, and I was very weak when I saw all of you. My favorite feeder was empty, so I had to leave quickly to find nectar somewhere else."

"Oh, we didn't know," says the flock quietly.

"I'm afraid you have it all wrong turkeys. We look forward to your visits. Please come back and have some more water," Bun-Bun pleads with the flock.

"We will!" cheer all the turkeys.

"Thank you for giving us the whole story. Next time we will ask and not guess what's going on," the eldest turkey promises.

It's easy to take another critter's behavior personally and think that it must be all about you. You might not know what's going on in a critter's life. Make sure you hear the full story before you jump to the wrong conclusion.

A Kitten Named Bounce

It's normal for young, growing critters to experiment with different styles, behaviors, and interests. In their search, critters sometimes go from one extreme to the other until they find what is right for them.

Here comes Bounce, a friendly and feisty black and white kitten, heading into the Perry's garden. The songbirds, mice, and Little Squirrel gather around her in the garden and notice that Bounce looks different today.

"What's with the slicked back, greasy fur?" the songbirds ask.

35

"Oh, it's a new style. Do you like it?" Bounce purrs.

"It's okay, if that's what you want. We barely recognized you," the songbirds reply.

"I've been doing a lot of thinking lately, and I'm going to be making some changes," Bounce says.

"What do you mean? all the critters ask eagerly.

"Starting today, no more chasing mice for me. I will only chase the wind!" she declares.

One of the mice stammers, "What did you say? No more chasing us?

But we like running from you. It's fun!"

"Chasing mice is for silly kittens. And I'm not a silly kitten anymore," says Bounce firmly.

"And no more boring naps either! Naps are for babies, and I'm not a baby."

"When kittens don't take naps, they are mean and grumpy," frets Little Squirrel, beginning to pace. "I get the jitters just thinking about a kitten that hasn't had her nap."

"Well, I'm a big kitten now," Bounce says. "No more dull fur, no more chasing mice, and no more boring naps."

The critters stare at Bounce in disbelief.

"Okay Bounce if that's what you want," the critters respond.

Bounce leaps into the air to chase the wind, galloping up and down and out of the garden.

Later, when the sun begins to set, Bounce slowly and quietly returns to the Perry's garden.

"I'm back," Bounce meows softly.

She's exhausted. All the critters gather around her.

"I learned a few things today," Bounce sighs, lying down on her side to stretch. "I like my silky coat better without so much grease. I want to use a little on my fur to make it shiny, but not slick and sticky. All kinds of things stuck to me today."

"Okay Bounce," the songbirds sing.

"And I discovered that I prefer chasing something that I can actually see. I can't see the wind. So, I'd like to go back to our kitty-chase-mice game," Bounce says.

"You bet!" the mice cheer.

"Well, I'm a big kitten now, and I have many things to do, so I might not have as much time to chase you as I did before," Bounce adds.

"That's okay," say the mice.

Bounce yawns and continues to stretch. "Another thing I learned today is that I do want a nap. I might not take as many naps as I did before, but I will NEVER give them up."

"I'm so glad to hear that!" Little Squirrel says, finally able to relax and stop pacing.

As Bounce curls up to go to sleep, she says to the critters around her, "I know I've been acting unusual lately. I haven't been myself. Thank you for being understanding and patient with me."

"That's what friends are for," the critters lovingly remind her.

Bounce will go in different directions as she grows and her interests change. She might go to the extreme sometimes, but if she listens to herself, she'll figure out what's right for her.

The Expert Nest Builders

It's natural to want to help others and see them succeed and do their best. But giving help to others needs to be done in a thoughtful way. Trying to force our ideas and behaviors on others does not work, as Mr. and Mrs. Quail learn during this year's week of nest building.

It's that time of year in the Perry's garden when all the birds begin to prepare for the arrival of their eggs. They are gathering materials and looking for a place to build their nests. As in the past few years, they are also preparing themselves for the arrival of Mr. and Mrs. Quail who think they are expert nest builders.

Every year Mr. and Mrs. Quail offer up many suggestions, which the other birds find annoying and bossy, on the right way to build a nest. And each year Mr. and Mrs. Quail find themselves baffled and frustrated as to why none of the other birds have adopted their techniques. After last years fighting Mr. and Mrs. Quail have decided to take a different approach. This year they will stand back and offer only encouragement and support.

"Here come the *expert nest builders*," Father Dove chirps sarcastically as Mr. and Mrs. Quail enter the garden. "I'm sure they will have lots of suggestions for us again this year. They don't think we know how to build a nest. It's very annoying," he mutters.

"Good morning doves," Mr. Quail chirps. "What a nice pile of materials you have gathered. That cotton you found will be an excellent addition to your nest."

"Hey, if you don't mind, we could do without all your nest-building tips this year," Father Dove blurts out.

"Oh no, you won't hear a chirp from us. I'm sure your nest will be just fine," Mr. Quail says as he and Mrs. Quail walk away, winking at each other.

"Did you hear what Mr. Quail said?" spouts Father Dove to anyone who will listen. "Who's he kidding? They won't be able to contain themselves. Not tell me how to build my nest... impossible! What's going on with those two anyway, complimenting me on my cotton?"

For the next week, all the birds in the garden peacefully gather supplies and busily construct their nests. There is no nagging or criticizing from Mr. or Mrs. Quail. At the end of the week, the birds go around the garden to look at the completed nests.

Mr. and Mrs. Quail approach Father Dove. "What a lovely nest you made. Great job!" Mr. and Mrs. Quail say cheerfully.

Father Dove stands back proudly. "Thank you," he replies. "Actually, without spending our energy on defending our nest-building skills, we had

44

time to observe how you make your nest so safe and warm. This year, we tried some of your past suggestions on our nests."

"I'm so glad you did, Father Dove. We never meant to be bossy. All we really wanted to do was help," Mr. Quail explains.

"Well, you did help. But not by nagging and bragging like you did in the past," Father Dove replies.

"We're pleased that we learned the right way to help," Mrs. Quail adds.

"Now, I'm already looking forward to next year," Father Dove cheers.

"We are too!" chirp Mr. and Mrs. Quail excitedly.

"So are we!" chime the rest of the birds in the garden.

Mr. and Mrs. Quail came to realize that bragging and bossy behavior doesn't help anyone. Instead, sometimes it's better to step back, offer encouragement, and do the best job you can for others to see. They just might follow your lead.

Be Careful What You Wish For

Wishes are wonderful things to have. But, when we desire something we do not have, we can lose sight of what is good in our own lives. Braveheart, the chicken, and Raccoon Jr. spend lots of time wishing for what the other one has, and not too much time on what the fulfillment of that wish looks like. Find out what happens when they finally get their wish.

As the sun begins to set, Mother, Raven, and Braveheart march to the side of the house and into their coop. After the chickens are inside, Mr. Perry closes and locks the gate to the coop.

"I can't wait to hear the night-time critters," cries Braveheart to Mother and Raven. "It always sounds like they're having a party, laughing and splashing in the pond. I don't want to be cooped up all night," Braveheart whines. "I want to be like Raccoon

Jr. I wish I was out there in the garden with the night-time critters having fun and roaming around."

"Shush!" Mother squawks. "It's time to sleep."

Braveheart settles into a corner when she sees Raccoon Jr. and his buddies pass the coop on their nightly run to gather food.

"What a sweet set up that is," says Raccoon Jr., admiring the coop. "I want to be like the chickens. I'd never need to hunt for food again. It looks comfortable and safe in the coop too. No critter could bother me in there."

Braveheart wishes she was OUT of the coop, while Raccoon Jr. wishes he was IN the coop.

"Hey, Raccoon, come here," Braveheart whispers from inside the coop. "I heard what you said, and I have an idea. Let's trade

places! Tomorrow, as the sun sets, you sneak into the coop, and I'll hide in the garden until the gate to the coop is locked. If you're sly, Mr. Perry will think you're one of the chickens. Then we both can get our wish."

"Great idea," Raccoon Jr. says. "Make sure you tell Mother and Raven

about our plan. I don't want to scare them when they see me in the coop instead of you."

"Oh my gosh! Good thinking. I'll let them know," replies Braveheart.

The next evening, Raccoon Jr. sneaks into the coop while Braveheart hides in the garden until the coop is locked. Their plan worked!

Free to roam, Braveheart wanders through the garden unsure of what to do. It's a lot colder out here than she expected. Her feathers are getting wet from the sprinklers and night-time dew.

"I'm hungry," Braveheart says, shivering. "Where are the bugs I like to eat? The bugs must be sleeping. And there's no water dish," she pouts. "Out here the night-time critter noises sound more like a fight than a party!"

Braveheart tries to calm herself, bracing for a long, sleepless night.

Meanwhile, in the secure and comfortable coop, Raccoon Jr. paces back and forth.

"How can chickens eat the same crackle day after day? Every night I hunt and catch something different to eat," he says to Mother and Raven who are huddled together in the corner with their eyes wide open.

After about an hour, Raccoon Jr. fumes, "Don't you feel trapped being locked up like this? I never sleep at this time of night."

Raccoon Jr. tries to calm himself, bracing for a long, restless night.

In the morning, as soon as the gate to the coop opens, Raccoon Jr.dashes OUT and Braveheart races IN. They smile as they pass each other, both happy to be back where they belong.

Braveheart and Raccoon Jr. will always remember the night they got their wish and then wished they hadn't. Both realized that what they already have is a blessing and gained a new appreciation for their own lives. It's good to have wishes and wise to think them through.

Goldie Finds a New Path

Critters have routines and can get used to things being a certain way. But things do change, and critters need to be flexible. Here is a story of how a goldfinch named Goldie learned that he could still get to where he wanted to go, even if the path he was used to had changed.

The Perry's garden is always an adventure, especially for visiting critters. The garden changes from season to season and sometimes even from day to day. Fences are often moved and potted flowers and plants are switched around. With all these changes, critters have to stay alert.

"Can we go to the Perry's garden again today? They have the best bird feeders!" chirps a large flock of goldfinches to their leader, the eldest goldfinch.

"Sure we can. Just be careful landing. Mr. Perry was working in the garden so things might not be in the same place as they were yesterday," the eldest goldfinch chirps back.

The flock of goldfinches fly to the Perry's garden. One by one they adjust their route and land next to the feeders. Goldie, the youngest, is the last one to enter the garden. He lands in the same spot he had landed in yesterday.

Without looking up, Goldie walks toward the feeders taking the same path he used the day before. Confused by the unfamiliar surroundings, Goldie quickly begins to panic.

"Where am I?" he cries out. Without looking up, Goldie begins pacing left and right anxiously looking for the path that was there yesterday. "What happened?"

The other goldfinches do not answer. They have already found a new path to the feeders and are busy munching away.

Goldie flutters his wings and flies forward. Still trying to use the same path he was on yesterday. But today there is a wire fence in his way. He continues to fly forward, only to be stopped again by the wire fence.

"Help! I'm stuck here!" Goldie shouts. "Where's the path I took yesterday? Why is this fence here? I can't get to the feeders!" he frets.

"Goldie, listen! You have to adjust your route today and find a new path," his goldfinch friends yell back. "Like we did. But first you have to calm down."

"What? A new path?" Goldie asks, confused. He stops flailing, takes a deep breath, and finally looks up. "Oh, now I see what you mean," he says relieved. "I can get to the feeders. I just have to fly *over* the fence."

So Goldie flies over the fence and lands next to his friends at the bird feeders.

"What took you so long?" the goldfinches tease.

Goldie laughs along with his friends, eager to join them for lunch.

Goldie was so intent on taking the same path to the feeders that the new fence startled him. His panic kept him from taking a moment to adjust to his new surroundings. When Goldie finally did stop and look up, he was able to see the new path to get to his destination. It was right in front of him. Things might change around us, but we can still get where we want to go, if we remain calm and flexible.

Little Glitter Duck

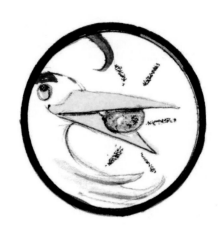

When critters act in ugly ways, it makes them look ugly to those around them. And when critters are beautiful on the inside, being kind to others and trying their best, it adds to their outer beauty. One spring Little Glitter Duck and all the critters in the Perry's garden experience what true beauty means.

The excitement around Mother Duck's nest was growing by the day. Inside her nest were three eggs. One of the eggs was the most amazing color the critters in the garden had ever seen. It was several shades of the lightest blue swirled together softly with what looked like glitter sprinkled in. The egg sparkled.

All the critters could talk about was the beautiful blue, glittery egg.

"Has it hatched yet?" ask the turtles, who make the long, slow trek to the duck's nest every day.

"What do you think the baby duck in the blue, sparkling shell will look like?" the squirrel family asks, so curious and full of anticipation.

"Will it be as beautiful as its shell?" the bunny family wonders.

After several weeks of waiting, the critters get their answer when the eggs finally hatch. The three baby ducks are all beautiful, but the littlest duck from the blue sparkling egg is quite different and especially majestic. She has the shiniest, softest fur, which will eventually become lovely feathers. She shimmers with glitter. And that becames her name, Little Glitter Duck.

All the critters crowd around, wanting to see and touch her. But Little Glitter Duck is overwhelmed by the attention. The critters are going to have to wait to meet her, she decides as she quickly waddles away and hides.

Shortly after the ducks are born, the turtle family makes its way slowly to the pond where Little Glitter Duck is swimming. It's her favorite thing to do.

"Hi!" the turtles say, trying to get Little Glitter Duck's attention. "We are the turtle family. The pond is one of our favorite spots in the Perry's garden. We love to swim, just like you do!"

Little Glitter Duck's reaction isn't nice.

"I would prefer that you don't swim in the pond when I'm in it. You are all very slow walkers, and I bet you swim slow too," Little Glitter Duck quacks loudly, quickly turning and paddling away.

"Well, I have never seen such rude behavior!" Mother Turtle exclaims. "Let's go."

Shocked, the turtle family walks away from the pond as the squirrel family approaches, anxiously wanting to meet Little Glitter Duck.

"Hello, Little Glitter Duck. We're so happy to finally meet you!" says Mother Squirrel. "These are my three children. I'm sure you will have lots of fun playing together. They can show you around the garden."

"I have no interest in making friends right now," Little Glitter Duck quacks loudly.

Shocked, the squirrel family scurries away from the pond as the bunny family approaches, anxiously wanting to meet Little Glitter Duck.

"Good afternoon, Little Glitter Duck! It's so good to meet you. We're the bunny family and have been waiting for you and your brother and sister to arrive. Your feathers are majestic! May we touch them?" asks Mother Bunny, reaching out to touch her.

"Do not touch my feathers!" Little Glitter Duck quacks loudly as she swims to the other side of the pond.

The frightened bunny family scatters throughout the garden.

A week passes, and all the critters' curiosity about Little Glitter Duck fades. They are saddened by her unfriendly behavior. Soon, an interesting thing starts to happen. With every snotty word or action Little Glitter Duck makes, the glitter on her feathers slowly fades and then seems to disappear.

"No one comes to see me anymore or asks me to come out and play," sulks Little Glitter Duck. "What happened?"

Little Glitter Duck catches a glimpse of herself in the reflection of the Perry's porch window. She can't see the glitter on her feathers. Where did it go?

"That's why they don't like me. I'm not majestic anymore!" she cries.

Looking on, Mother Duck decides it's time to have a chat with her Little Glitter Duck.

"No little one, it's because of what is coming out of you that makes them stay away. Right now they

can't see past your snotty, rude behavior to notice your glitter. That's why you can't even see it. Why don't you try being kind and friendly, then see what happens?" Mother Duck says gently.

"I didn't want to be mean and push them away," says Little Glitter Duck. "I was embarrassed by all the attention. Everyone always wanting to touch me. I didn't know what to say or how to react. I guess that wasn't very nice."

For the next few weeks, Little Glitter Duck sets out to make things right. She works at showing the critters how sorry she is through her kind words and helpful behavior.

"Thank you for turtle-sitting while I hunted for food," Mother Turtle says to Little Glitter Duck. "It was very helpful to me."

"It's my pleasure. I really like your turtle babies. They are fun to be with," Little Glitter Duck replies.

"Thank you Little Glitter Duck for watching our pile of acorns while we hid the rest of our food. That was very kind of you," the squirrel family calls out as they scurry up their tree.

"I'm glad to help!" Little Glitter Duck calls back so they can hear.

"Thank you for the basket of carrots and lettuce!" the bunny family tells Little Glitter Duck.

"Seeing them made me think of you and your family. I hope they were yummy," Little Glitter Duck replies.

"They were!" says the bunny.

Little Glitter Duck apologizes to all the critters in the garden and asks for a new start, which they kindly give her. It takes a while, but slowly, with her many kind actions and a change in attitude, Little Glitter Duck's feathers begin to sparkle and shimmer once again, for everyone to see.

After Little Glitter Duck figured out how to be good on the inside, her outside beauty followed. The glitter on her feathers was never really gone, but it was hidden by her meanness, which the critters could not see past. When we act in ugly ways, it makes us look ugly to those around us. Beauty, truly comes from the inside.

Sights and Sounds of Nature

From the morning bird
who lets us know that the day is beginning
to the last bits of light from the setting sun,
each day brings a beautiful nature show
of sights and sounds for us to enjoy.

I love to hear
the birds chirping, the turkeys gobbling,
the splashing of rain or a waterfall,
the wind playing with the leaves.

I love to see
a group of squirrels playing,
a deep blue sky filled with fluffy white clouds
or wisps of red and yellow,
birds flying, a flower blooming.

I do not need to know exactly
where everything comes from
to be thankful for the wonder of it all.

Nature is always waiting for us to notice it,
ready to offer up delight, peace, beauty,
and entertainment.

Whenever you can, sit quietly outside.
Take a deep breath and be still.

Nature will come to you.

Open your eyes and ears
and let all of nature surround you.

Say, "Thank You! Thank You! Thank you!"

When I am with nature, I am happy.

I hope you are too!

About the Author

Sondra Perry lives in San Ramon, California, with her husband Lance, and Henry, a great blue heron who has been visiting for over twelve years. Her first book, *The Most Unusual Pet Ever: Henry Our Great Blue Heron and His Adventures,* is the true story of meeting Henry the Heron and their continued friendship. Sondra's second book, (first in the Kids Carrots Book Series), *Baby Carrots,* was released in 2014. This is the second book in the series. Look for the third book, *Kids Carrots,* out in 2018. Sondra is available for fun and educational readings and presentations to groups of all ages. You can reach her at *sondraperry@comcast.net*

About the Illustrator

Award-winning artist Janice Byer has a Bachelor of Fine Arts degree from the California College of Arts and Crafts. She is a successful watercolor, pastel, and oil painter. Visit her online at www.artistjanicebyer.com

More Books by Sondra Perry

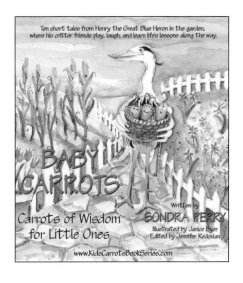

Please visit

www.KidsCarrotsBookSeries.com

or

www.HenryTheGreatBlueHeron.com

for more information and pictures.
Friend "HenryBlueHeron" on Facebook
Follow Henry on Twitter, @HenryBlueHeron

Thanks for reading *Crunchy Carrots!*